HICKORY

THIS IS A NEW YORK REVIEW BOOK
PUBLISHED BY THE NEW YORK REVIEW OF BOOKS
435 Hudson Street, New York, NY 10014
www.nyrb.com

Library of Congress Cataloging-in-Publication Data
Brown, Palmer.
Hickory / by Palmer Brown.
p. cm. — (New York Review children's collection)
Summary: An indoor mouse ventures into the outside world and finds true
friendship.
ISBN 978-1-59017-627-6 (alk. paper)
[1. Mice—Fiction. 2. Friendship—Fiction.] I. Title.
PZ7.B816647Hi 2013
[E]—dc23
2012035498

ISBN 978-1-59017-627-6

Cover design by Louise Fili Ltd.

Printed in the United States on acid-free paper.
3 5 7 9 10 8 6 4 2

HICKORY

BY

PALMER BROWN

THE NEW YORK REVIEW
CHILDREN'S COLLECTION
New York

HICKORY

CHAPTER ONE

IN THE CLOCK

ALFWAY up the stairs of an old farmhouse, on the broad landing, bright with rose-patterned carpet, stood a tall grandfather clock, ticking time away. Its face had painted on it a sad-eyed moon which moved with the days of the month. Partway down the front of the walnut case there was a round glass window, so that you could watch the brass pendulum swing and see it tick. And, because there was a hole near one of the feet at the back of the clock, in the bottom there lived a family of mice.

Since the mother mouse had a sense of humor, she named her three little mice Hickory, Dickory and Dock. Their father would have preferred more dignified names, but after going through the list from Abraham to Zachary, he found it easier to agree than to decide which names were dignified enough, and he loved his mice anyway.

Of the three, Hickory was the biggest, and the liveliest too. He could ride the pendulum the longest without getting dizzy, and he could shinny up the weight-chains into the clockworks without getting his tail pinched in the wheels. Only Hickory dared to stay in the works when the hour struck and the chime

made every cog quiver. His brother, Dickory, always ran down. His sister, Dock, would not go up at all.

"I do not want cobwebs in my whiskers," she said.

"They are your whiskers," Hickory answered. He never teased. However, he cautioned his brother always to give the pendulum an extra push when he was through swinging.

"Why?" Dickory asked.

"If we stop the clock," Hickory said, "the farmer will investigate, and he may find us."

Once a week the old farmer would unlock a door in the front of the clock to wind it, but he never bothered to look down. His wife was

old too, and the bottom of the clock was one of the places she did not dust any more. Sometimes their cat would sniff the carpet near the clock, but since she was then either going downstairs to eat or upstairs to sleep, she never lingered. For their part, the mice were careful.

"Eat all you want," the father said, "but never leave paw-prints in the butter." They never did.

Every year, in early fall, the farmer's wife would set a few rickety mousetraps in the kitchen—"to catch those field-mice coming in for the winter," she said. She never caught one of the field-mice, who avoided mechanical contraptions, but once she nearly caught Hickory,

4

who thought he knew everything about traps and wanted to do what he could to make life less dangerous. He liked to prowl the pantry, springing the set traps with a piece of broom-straw. A snapped trap made a fine clatter, bringing the farmer's wife running to see what she had not caught. Sometimes, too, the bait was worth sampling. Usually it was raw bacon rind, which Hickory detested.

Unluckily this time– it was just after Thanksgiving Day– the farmer's wife baited the trap with crisp turkey skin, which was much more inviting. Perhaps because he was

too eager or used too short a broomstraw, Hickory got one of his feet pinched. After his mother and father pried him loose with a clothes-pin, he insisted that the trap went off without his even touching it. This was not exactly true, but it made it hurt less to say so.

The turkey skin was put to good use. Hickory's mother rubbed the fat from it on his bruised toes, and she tied up his foot in a scrap

of red wool. She made him stay in the clock for a full week, although the last two days she let him swing on the pendulum for exercise. His father made him a crutch out of two toothpicks and a match-stick, and his mother made a pad for it of blue calico. Hickory was pleased with it, hobbling about long after he needed it, and he snapped all the traps with it to get even.

CHAPTER TWO

A TIME TO GO

HE FIELD-MICE who wintered in the farmhouse were impressed with Hickory's crutch. They were delicate old mice who found the winter too hard in the fields, and the blue tunnels under the snow too cold on their feet. They liked to sun themselves in the thin winter light on a south cellar window-sill among the geraniums. It made them feel at home a little, although they complained that the farmer's wife ought to have potted more sensible plants, like wild strawberries. The geraniums were

too spicy and gave them indigestion.

For the field-mice Hickory invented stories about life in the farmhouse. When he told them about a frightened mouse that ran into a Swiss cheese just before the farmer's wife began to slice it, Hickory crashed his crutch down as he said, "And she cut another slice, and another, and another!" The field-mice ran squealing before he could finish, covering their ears and hiding in a feather duster, so he did not need to make up an end to the story.

Hickory's brother said, "It is not fair to begin a story without knowing the end."

His sister said, "Anyone can guess the ending."

His mother said, "I do not want to hear it if

9

the ending is sad."

His father said, "All stories have their endings in their beginnings, if you know where to look."

It was the field-mice who were responsible for Hickory's leaving home. They were forever saying how much better things were in their beloved fields. The air was more salubrious, the nights more restful. Their noses did not dry out so. They never had twinges in the tips of their tails. The farmer's best baked bread could never match the flavor of wheat gnawed from the husk. The finest red raspberry jam was tasteless compared to the sunlit blackberry bursting on the bramble.

"It is a wonderful place," the oldest field-mouse said. "Each blade of grass you pull has a sweet white nibble at the base, each honeysuckle flower a drop of nectar."

So Hickory went, not with the field-mice, but alone, after they had gone in the spring when the lilacs bloomed. His father approved and said he hoped it would make a mouse of him. His mother did not like to see him go, but she pretended that she was glad. She sighed and said, "I remember a field once,

all full of blue violets, and a yellow bird singing." She hoped that Hickory would settle himself in the upper meadow, because she could see it from the corner of the stairway window, watching from between the organdie curtain and the pane.

"I will," he promised.

The day Hickory left, his sister gave him some anise seeds in a knapsack made of

brown linen, in case he got a sore throat, and a clove in case he had a toothache. His brother gave him a pink rubber tip for his crutch, gnawed out of a pencil eraser. Both gifts were supposed to be secrets, but Hickory knew about them, because his sister upset the farmer's wife's sewing-basket looking for the linen, and because his brother had been picking bits of rubber out of his teeth for a week.

His father gave him a lecture and said, "Here you know what the dangers are, and snapping traps is mostly a game, but in the meadow there may be traps of a different sort. Owls, for instance, and– why, you have never even gotten your feet wet."

"Oh! Wet feet!" his mother cried. "Maybe we should not let him go after all."

"Nonsense," his father said. "I just want him to know that life is not going to be all cake-crumbs and cheese-parings."

Hickory's mother kissed him then and said, "If you get lonesome, remember we love you and want you back."

"Oh, there will be too much to do to get lonesome," Hickory said.

There was a sharp click in the clockworks, which always meant that the hour was about to strike. As he often did, Hickory's father recited along with the chime:

> Time is going,
> Never staying,
> Always flowing,
> Ever saying:
> Gone!

It was one o'clock and time to go.

CHAPTER THREE

IN THE MEADOW

ICKORY left the farmhouse by way of a hole under the cellar door, which is how the field-mice came and went. He also took their advice in heading first for the barn. It was a convenient place, they had told him, to break their journey to the meadow. But the barn smelled of chickens and pigs, so Hickory decided not to stay.

"Is the meadow this way?" he asked a barn-mouse, who looked grubby from the chaff.

"On up the hill," the barn-mouse said. "But why anyone wants to go up there, when the hay here is all cut and dried… It's lonely up there. Nothing but beetles to talk to."

"What do beetles talk about?" Hickory asked.

"Beetle business, I suppose. Burrowing holes in the dark. I never bother with them," the barn-mouse said.

Hickory noticed that the barn-mouse's whiskers were bent from peering around corners. He thanked him, inviting him to visit the farmhouse sometime. Running up the hill, Hickory sang the old song:

How many miles to Babylon?
Three score miles and ten.
Can I get there by candle-light?
Yes, and back again.

But he did not think he would ever want to go back.

Long before he reached the meadow, the heavy honeysuckle smell spilling down the hillside told him he was headed right. It was dark when he crept through the warm stones of the meadow wall. He continued far into the open field before he stopped beside a large rock under which a rabbit had once begun to burrow a hole and then had changed its mind. After poking in the hole with his crutch to make sure there were no beetles in it, Hickory lay down in it with a red clover bloom for a pillow. For a long time he could not get to sleep. He missed the ticking of the clock.

In the morning Hickory had a fit of sneezing, mostly from the clover pillow, but he took one of his anise seeds to be safe, and he went out of the hole to get the lay of the land. The gray

rock, rusted with lichens, stood in the middle of the meadow. Because the rock was too big to move, the farmer had always plowed around it, but for many years the field had not been used, and a blueberry bush had grown beside the rock. Half buried nearby lay an empty pickle jar someone had thrown at the rock and missed. It reminded Hickory of the pantry in the farmhouse.

From the top of the rock Hickory could see the whole meadow, a wilderness of weeds and wild flowers. Beyond the meadow lay the lower pasture, which he had crossed, and beyond that the red barn, and finally the farmhouse, looking no bigger than a match-box.

Hickory located the stairway window, and he waved. In the other direction, to the south, the hillside rose in woodland, quiet and dark. Out in the meadow a brown-and-yellow grasshopper sang:

> My life is but a summer song,
> A little carol in the sun.

Hickory waved at the grasshopper as she flew past, her underwings flashing pink, and the grasshopper waved back a welcome. Hickory took it as a good sign. He would stay here.

CHAPTER FOUR

FINDING A FRIEND

O IMPROVE the rabbit hole, Hickory dug out a bedroom and he lined it with thistle-down. Up against the bottom of the rock he rounded out cubby-holes for seeds and grasses, so that he would not need to go out in bad weather. For fun he burrowed a tunnel to the pickle jar to use as a sun parlor on cool days, and in it he planted a wild strawberry. He found a hickory nut without a worm-hole in it, and he buried it beside his doorway for good luck, and it grew.

As he did his chores Hickory sang a song his
mother used to sing tidying up the clock:

A LITTLE house, a little room,
To keep it swept, a little broom,

A little carpet on the floor,
A little curtain at the door,

A little bed, a little chest,
A little chair, to muse and rest,

A little larder, snug and tight,
A little lamp, when it is night,

A little table and, oh, please!
A little bread, a little cheese.

The song made him think of his family. He wondered how they were, and whether Dickory was snapping the traps, or whether Dock now dared to climb into the clockworks. Now that he was settled, there was not much to do except to sit in his doorway and listen to the hum of the meadow. He felt that he was happy, and yet something was missing. The field-mice were too busy with their own affairs to be much company. He was lonely and wanted someone to talk to— even a beetle, about beetle business.

One afternoon, when the air was drowsy with meadowsweet, as Hickory sat watching a striped caterpillar in the blueberry bush, too busy eating leaves to have time for conversa-

tion, he heard the grasshopper break off her singing to cry "Look out!" Hickory knew the grasshopper meant him, and he tumbled through his doorway just an as orange barn-cat leaped down from the top of his rock. Hickory ran into his deepest tunnel, halfway to the pickle jar, and the cat reached a paw as far as she could into his parlor.

When he felt a little braver, he went into the pickle jar to shake his crutch at the cat, but the grasshopper flew over the jar, saying, "Lie low, so the cat can't see you, and I'll take care of her." The grasshopper teased the cat, hopping first this way and then that, leading her across the meadow into a thicket of thistles by the farthest wall.

The next day, before the wild morning-glories had crumpled or the dew had dried, with wet feet Hickory went looking for the grasshopper among the blossoming milkweed and wild carrot.

"I want to thank you for leading the cat away," he said. "I'm glad I found you."

"Don't ever eat milkweed. It tastes terrible," the grasshopper remarked, and then she answered, "It was nothing. Here in the meadow we do what we can to help one another. Besides, it was fun."

"Like snapping traps," Hickory said.

He and the grasshopper soon became good

friends, and now he knew that what had been missing from the meadow was someone to share it with. The grasshopper's name was Hope, so Hickory called her Hop for short. Together they went exploring, and they discovered the sweetness of blackberries and the sharpness of sassafras twigs. They learned useful things– that chicory is bitter, but sorrel only sour. And they learned useless things too – that the track of a snail is silver winding

through the grass, but the light of a firefly is green gold melting in the air. Hop said that before summer was done she would have Hickory jumping like a grasshopper. Once he took her through his house, but she only said, "It makes me restless to be underground."

"Why?" Hickory asked.

"I came from the ground," she said, "and someday I will go back to it, but not before I have to."

CHAPTER FIVE

THE END OF A SONG

N A DAY in late summer, when the goldenrod was fading and the air smelled of apples, Hickory was gathering rose hips when he heard familiar voices shouting, "Surprise! Surprise!" His father and mother and brother had come for the day to visit him and to have a picnic. His sister had recently married a barn-mouse– the one with the bent whiskers– and the family brought a piece of the wedding-cake and a licorice gumdrop and a piece of Hickory's favorite sharp cheese, all packed in a woven sweet-grass thimble-case used for a picnic basket.

Hickory brought out his best seeds and berries, and everyone tasted a little of everything, including catnip for the digestion. The oldest field-mouse, who had sniffed out the cheese, invited herself. Hop came too and was polite about tasting the cheese. Hickory told his family how Hop had rescued him from the cat, and he demonstrated some grasshopper jumps, pretending he had wings.

"I knew a cricket once," Hickory's mother said to Hop, to be saying something.

"It jumped in the apple-butter crock and drowned," Hickory's father interrupted. "So I hope you have taught Hickory better jumping than that."

When it was time to go, Hickory's father shook paws with him, and Hickory felt very grown-up. His mother started to kiss him, but he leaned aside instead to pick up for her the thimble-case now filled with rose hips, and she understood. Dickory, who had seemed shy and quiet all afternoon, said, "So long, Hick," and tweaked his tail as he used to. They were still his family.

Hop offered to lead them as far as the meadow wall. Watching them go, the oldest field-mouse said to Hickory, "I think you must love that grasshopper very much."

"I do," Hickory answered.

"You will miss her then, come frost," she said, pinching up the last crumb of cheese and smoothing her whiskers.

"What do you mean?" Hickory asked.

"Oh, didn't you know?" she said as she left. "Just ask Hop to sing her little song through to the end sometime."

Hickory wondered whether Hop would be

leaving the meadow. It would not be much fun
without her.

For several days after the picnic Hickory did
not see Hop. He thought that perhaps the
cheese had disagreed with her. The nights
turned cool, and the crickets' chirping grew
thin and shrill. Weeds were wet with dew until
noon, and poison-ivy leaves turned an ugly red.
Hickory needed no clock to tell him that time
was passing. Then one warm afternoon he
heard Hop singing again, but without much
spirit:

> My life is but a summer song,
> A little carol in the sun.

"Go on, Hop," Hickory called to her, partly
to cheer her up, but mostly because he was
curious. "Let's hear the rest of your song."

Hop began again and sang straight through:

> My life is but a summer song,
> A little carol in the sun.
> Now, when the nights grow cold and long,
> The song I sing will soon be done.

As Hop finished, Hickory began to cry. Now he knew that when cold weather came at last, the grasshopper would die.

"We must do something!" he said.

"I'm afraid there isn't much we can do," Hop answered. "That's the way things are."

Hickory pointed out that Hop could stay with him.

"Not in a hole in the ground. I could not live without the sun," she said.

31

"What about the pickle jar?" Hickory asked. "You could eat the strawberries."

Hop said there was not enough room there to stretch her legs.

"Then we'll go back to the farmhouse," Hickory said.

"And land in the apple-butter crock?" Hop asked. She did agree to sleep that night beside the rock, because it held the heat after the sun had set. In his warm bedroom Hickory dreamed of Swiss cheese and a knife.

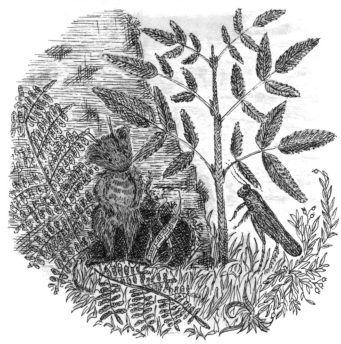

CHAPTER SIX

A JOURNEY BEGUN

HE NEXT morning Hickory found that in the night all the leaves had fallen from his hickory tree. Some of them had covered Hop, but she was still so cold that Hickory gave her his last anise seed to take away the chill.

A yellow bird perched in a sweetbrier to watch. "Go south," she said, "where it is always warm."

An orange butterfly resting on a gentian said,
"Go south, like us, before the killing frost."
Hickory tossed his crutch in the air. "That's

35

it, Hop!" he cried. "We'll go south too and find some sunny meadow there."

Hop asked the yellow bird, "Is it far to go?" but the bird was gone.

"Is it hard to find?" she called after the orange butterfly. The butterfly was already too far away to hear her.

"It does not matter," Hickory said. "South is south. We will find the way."

Hop asked, "You're not doing this just because of that business about the cat, are you?"

"No," Hickory said. "Being friends isn't just returning favors. Besides, I once heard, here in the meadow we do what we can to help."

The grasshopper was still troubled. "What about your house," she asked, "and all your things? You are happy here. I can go alone."

Hickory was sure that Hop could not get far by herself. Her wings were frayed, and she could scarcely fly. "The rock will be here when we get back," he said, "and the pickle jar too. My house is only a hole in the ground. It was here when I came. Maybe it will be a surprise for someone who needs it after we go."

So they went, and all Hickory took was his crutch, because there might be traps to snap.

At the wall they met the oldest field-mouse, who was getting ready to go back to the farmhouse.

"Frost will be early this year," she said. "I feel it in my whiskers." She was surprised that Hickory was leaving. "Whatever shall I tell your dear parents?" she asked.

"Tell them that I love them," Hickory said, "and that I will be good."

They left the meadow and entered the wood

and climbed the hill to the top. By then it was dark, and they slept in a clearing, curled up in woolly mullein leaves. Hickory covered his ears when he heard the owls hooting.

CHAPTER SEVEN

THE SOUND OF TIME

T DAYBREAK Hickory looked out from beneath the mullein leaves in wonder. "Is there frost?" Hop asked. It was not frost they saw, but thousands of wild asters, pink and purple and white, field after field, hill after hill, and in the distance the lower land and, far off, for the first time, the sea. They started down, together at first, until Hop limbered up. Then she hopped on ahead to pick out the easiest way.

39

A wedge of geese honked overhead, and milk-weed silk soared shimmering in the soft air.

Early in the afternoon they rested in an old orchard where wasps were eating holes in the brown rotting fallen pears.

"Hickory," Hop asked, "honestly, do you think we'll get there?"

With his crutch Hickory shooed away a yellow-jacket. "I think so," he said, not sure, never sure, but not afraid to hope.

"Let's sing something as we go," Hickory said, and he began, "How many miles to Babylon?"

Hop, who did not know that song, answered with the only song she knew. So they sang, each a line in turn:

How many miles to Babylon?
My life is but a summer song,
Three score miles and ten.
A little carol in the sun.
Can I get there by candle-light?
Now, when the nights grow cold and long,
Yes, and back again.
The song I sing will soon be done.

It made a sort of sense. Before them lay a hundred hills they might never climb and a hundred streams they might never cross, but they would try. Nearly out of sound a clock in a church steeple began to strike the hour. The chime was the same as the chime of the grandfather clock, and Hickory could almost hear his father repeating:

Time is going,
Never staying,
Always flowing,
Ever saying:
Gone!

He shivered. He would have liked to jam the clockworks with his crutch, but it would not have helped at all. He knew it, and without looking back he left his crutch in the tall grass.

As the sound of the chimes faded, Hop called back to Hickory, "What was that noise?"

"Nothing," Hickory answered, catching up. "Nothing but a clock striking one."

The sun was bright, and there was not a cloud in the sky, but the air was cool and dry and very still. That night on these owl-haunted upper ridges there would be hard frost.

PALMER BROWN (1919–2012) was born in Chicago and attended Swarthmore and the University of Pennsylvania. He was the author and illustrator of five books for children: *Something for Christmas*; *Beyond the Pawpaw Trees* and its sequel, *The Silver Nutmeg*; *Cheerful*; and *Hickory*—all published by The New York Review Children's Collection.

EILÍS DILLON
The Island of Horses
The Lost Island

ELEANOR FARJEON
The Little Bookroom

PENELOPE FARMER
Charlotte Sometimes

PAUL GALLICO
The Abandoned

RUMER GODDEN
An Episode of Sparrows
The Mousewife

LUCRETIA P. HALE
The Peterkin Papers

RUSSELL and LILLIAN HOBAN
The Sorely Trying Day

RUTH KRAUSS and MARC SIMONT
The Backward Day

MUNRO LEAF and ROBERT LAWSON
Wee Gillis

RHODA LEVINE and EDWARD GOREY
Three Ladies Beside the Sea
He Was There from the Day We Moved In

BETTY JEAN LIFTON and EIKOH-HOSOE
Taka-chan and I

NORMAN LINDSAY
The Magic Pudding